DINOFOURS™
WHERE'S MOMMY?

This book belongs to

Nastalé

For Aunt Beverly
— S.M.

Library of Congress Cataloging-in-Publication Data

Metzger, Steve.
  Where's Mommy? / by Steve Metzger; illustrated by Hans Wilhelm.
    p.   cm. — (Dinofours)
  Summary: When Danielle's mother is late picking her up at the end of the school day, her teacher takes her mind off the problem by making her part of the Super-Duper After-School Cleanup Crew.
  ISBN 0-590-37456-7
  [1. Nursery schools—Fiction.   2. Schools—Fiction.   3. Mother and child—Fiction.   4. Dinosaurs—Fiction.]
  I. Wilhelm, Hans, 1945-   ill.   II. Title.   III. Series: Metzger, Steve. Dinofours.
PZ7.M56775Wh   1997
[E]—dc21   97-9118
                                                                                               CIP
                                                                                                AC

10 9 8 7 6 5 4

Printed in the U.S.A.   24
First printing, November 1997

DINOFOURS™
WHERE'S MOMMY?

by Steve Metzger
Illustrated by Hans Wilhelm

Cartwheel
·B·O·O·K·S·®
SCHOLASTIC INC.
New York Toronto London Auckland Sydney

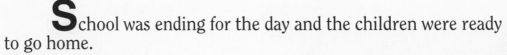

School was ending for the day and the children were ready to go home.

"Tomorrow," said Mrs. Dee, "we will play 'Duck, Duck, Goose' and bake alphabet pretzels."

"Great!" said Tara. "I love pretzels!"

"I love pretzels more than you do," exclaimed Brendan. "I love pretzels more than anyone in the whole world. One day, I ate a hundred million pretzels!"

"No, you didn't," said Tara.

"Yes, I did," said Brendan.

"Okay," said Mrs. Dee, looking up at the clock. "It's time to line up."

The parents, grandparents, and baby-sitters were waiting in the next room.

"Hi, Mommy," shouted Albert as he ran into his mother's arms.

"Hello, Grandpa," said Tracy. "Do you want to see my painting? It's a giant bird."

All the children excitedly found the adults who were there to pick them up—all except Danielle. She couldn't find her mother anywhere.

"Where's my mommy?" asked Danielle in a worried voice.

"Your mommy's on her way," said Mrs. Dee. "She'll be here in a little while."

"Is she OK?" Danielle asked. "Do you think something happened to her?"

"I'm sure she's fine," said Mrs. Dee. "Let's see if she called and left a message."

Mrs. Dee and Danielle went to the office. There were no messages from Danielle's mother.

"Your mommy is probably stuck in traffic," said Mrs. Dee. "Sometimes that happens."

Danielle sang this song to herself:

Where's Mommy? Where's Mommy?
I wish that she was near.
Where's Mommy? Where's Mommy?
I want her to be here!

Mrs. Dee put her arm around Danielle.

"You're a brave girl," said Mrs. Dee.

"Why?" asked Danielle.

"Because it's hard to wait for your mommy when all of the other children have been picked up from school," said Mrs. Dee.

That made Danielle feel a little better. But she still missed her mother.

"All right!" said Mrs. Dee in a cheery voice. "Let's find something for you to do."

Mrs. Dee and Danielle walked back inside their classroom.

"What shall it be?" asked Mrs. Dee. "Do you want to build with blocks, draw a picture, or listen to a story?"

"I want to draw a picture," Danielle said, sitting down at the art table.

Mrs. Dee gave her a box of crayons and a big piece of paper.

Danielle drew a picture of herself and her mommy at the zoo. When she finished, Danielle looked at the picture and began to cry.

Mrs. Dee sat in the chair next to her.

"Don't worry, Danielle," said Mrs. Dee. "I'm sure your mommy will be here very soon."

After a few moments, Danielle stopped crying.

"Am I still a brave girl?" sniffled Danielle.

"Yes, of course," said Mrs. Dee. "Crying has nothing to do with being brave."

"Really?" asked Danielle.

"Really!" answered Mrs. Dee.

Mrs. Dee stood up and looked at a nearby table.

"My, my, my," she said, shaking her head.

"What's wrong?" asked Danielle.

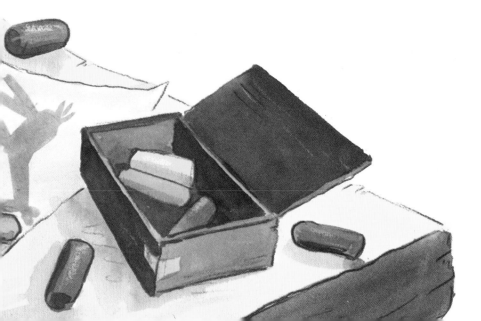

"Just look at this table!" said Mrs. Dee. "It's covered with mud dough. This is a job for the Super-Duper After-School Cleanup Crew!"

"What's the Super-Duper After-School Cleanup Crew?" Danielle asked.

"They're special workers who clean up classrooms when the school day is over," said Mrs. Dee.

Mrs. Dee put on a baseball cap from the dress-up area.

"Did you know that I'm a member of the Super-Duper After-School Cleanup Crew?" Mrs. Dee said as she filled up a bucket with warm, soapy water.

"No," said Danielle. "Can I be a member, too?"

"Oh, I don't know," said Mrs. Dee. "You have to be strong."

"I'm strong," said Danielle.

"And you have to like soapy water," said Mrs. Dee.

"I like soapy water," answered Danielle.

"Then, let's go!" said Mrs. Dee as she put a cap on Danielle's head and handed her a sponge.

Mrs. Dee and Danielle sang songs as they scrubbed the mud dough off the table.

Just as they finished, Danielle's mother walked into the classroom.

"I'm sorry I'm so late," said Danielle's mother. "I was stuck in a big traffic jam."

When Danielle saw her mother, she turned around and faced the other way.

"What's the matter?" asked Danielle's mother. "Aren't you glad to see me?"

Mrs. Dee walked over to Danielle's mother.

"I think she's a little upset that she had to wait for you," said Mrs. Dee.

Danielle's mother noticed Danielle's drawing on the art table. She picked it up to get a closer look.

"Who made this beautiful picture?" she asked.

"I did, Mommy!" said Danielle as she ran to her mother's side. "It's you and me! And we're at the zoo! See the giraffe and the lion! It's for you, Mommy! I missed you."

"I missed you, too, Danielle," said her mother.

Danielle and her mommy hugged each other for a long time.
"I was on the Super-Duper After-School Cleanup Crew,"
said Danielle. "And Mrs. Dee said I was a brave girl."
"I'm sure you were," said Danielle's mother.
Danielle smiled a great, big smile.

"I have a song for you, Mommy," she said. Danielle sang this song:

Mommy, when you didn't come,
I joined the Cleanup Crew.
But now I'm happy that you're here.
Mommy, I love you!

And then it was time to go home.